SCAREDY CATS

For Marmaduke, Shula and Harry.

Find out more about the Scaredy Cats
at Shoo's fabulous website:
www.shoo-rayner.co.uk

ORCHARD BOOKS
96 Leonard Street, London EC2A 4XD
Orchard Books Australia
32/45-51 Huntley Street, Alexandria, NSW 2015
First published in Great Britain in 2005
First paperback edition 2005
Copyright © Shoo Rayner 2005
The right of Shoo Rayner to be identified as the author
and illustrator of this work has been asserted by him in
accordance with the Copyright, Designs, and Patents Act, 1988.
A CIP catalogue record for this book is available
from the British Library.
ISBN 1 84362 445 1 (hardback)
ISBN 1 84362 744 2 (paperback)
1 3 5 7 9 10 8 6 4 2 (hardback)
1 3 5 7 9 10 8 6 4 2 (paperback)
Printed in Great Britain

The Killer Catflap

ShooRayner

The silver moon filled the back yard
as Purdy sneaked out of the café
where she lived. Something flew at her
from the shadows. It screamed loud
enough to wake the dead.

Purdy froze to the spot.

Pain shot through her body, as
the nightmare creature sank its
needle-sharp teeth into her leg.

With a fierce swipe of her paw, Purdy hurled her attacker across the yard. "Stay there!" she ordered.

Five minutes later, Purdy raced to
join her friends at the Secret Society
of Scaredy Cats.

"That Fergal," she sighed as she reached them. "I know he's only a kitten, but he never leaves me alone!"

"Ah! But he's such a sweet little thing!" chimed Molly.

"The trouble with kittens," said Max,
"is that they get bigger and bigger!"

"It's not just kittens that get bigger"
growled Kipling, their leader.

Silence fell upon the secret circle. Kipling's eyes narrowed into slits. He was ready to tell a story. The story they had all come to hear.

"This story is about my cousin's best friend, Parsnip," Kipling began. "She lived at Henry Lee's Roadside Restaurant."

There had always been one or two
cockroaches in the kitchen, and
Parsnip enjoyed catching them.
It was her job.

But after a long, hot summer the kitchen was infested with a new breed of huge and menacing cockroaches.

They were too fast to catch...

...and they ate absolutely everything.

Parsnip had nightmares. She would dream she was being eaten alive. When she woke, she would find herself surrounded by the skittering creatures. Their hairy feelers would quiver in the electric air.

Henry Lee put down poison, but the cockroaches were too clever for that old trick. They grew in number day by day.

The health inspector told Henry that
he had never seen cockroaches like
them before. Henry was going to need
some serious help.

The next day, the health inspector returned with a small black and yellow striped box. Inside was a lizard the size and colour of a french bean.

SUPER LIZARD

WARNING
THIS LIZARD
EATS A LOT!

"This little fellow is a cockroach-eating machine," the health inspector explained. "Just let him loose and he'll do the job."

19

Parsnip was amazed at how the tiny creature went straight to work. The lizard could change the colour of its skin. Perfectly disguised, it waited patiently for a cockroach to scuttle out from under the fridge.

In a flash, the lizard's tongue lashed out...flick-a-slick! A split second later, the roach's wriggling body was being crunched and munched in the lizard's powerful jaws.

Parsnip shivered with excitement. This tiny creature was her saviour. She was glad she was not a cockroach.

With every flick-a-slick, the lizard grew bigger. So did its appetite.

The lizard got better at disguising itself. It was uncanny — sometimes Parsnip walked right past the lizard, never knowing it was there.

Once, Parsnip watched a cockroach scuttle across the kitchen floor, when — flick-a-slick! — it disappeared in front of her eyes.

Parsnip looked to where she could hear the lizard crunching on the horrible insect. There was nothing there, except...maybe...

As she watched, the lizard appeared from nowhere, as if it were a photograph being developed. It swallowed hard, and fixed Parsnip with an empty stare...

The lizard showed no feeling.
It never slept, it just ate and grew
bigger by the day. Soon it was
bigger than Parsnip.

Finally, the day came when the kitchen was cockroach-free and Parsnip could sleep in peace once more.

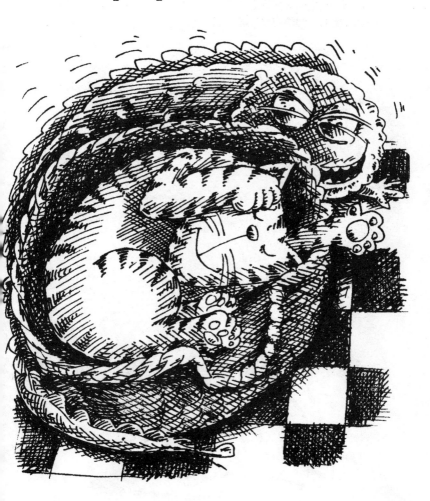

One night soon after, Parsnip woke
suddenly. She could hear the sound of
claws, slowly clicking across the hard
kitchen floor.

She heard a sticky noise, like lips being licked. But she couldn't see anything!

The moonlight shafted through the slatted windows, creating awkward shadows. Every nerve in her body tingled. She sensed danger.

The shadows surged around her like a rippling wave. Parsnip's heart thumped like a steam hammer. She edged towards the back door.

The lizard appeared out of thin air. Its hard, scaly mouth cracked into a sinister grin. Its horrible tongue flicked across its lips.

A thought raced through Parsnip's brain. "He's eaten all the cockroaches. What's he going to live on now?"

Without hesitating, Parsnip burst
through the catflap.

She thought she was safe until she
heard the hideous noise. Flick-a-slick!

Her cry of triumph quickly turned into a terrifying scream of fear. Fast as lightning, the cold, sticky tip of the lizard's tongue shot through the open catflap behind her and wrapped itself around her leg.

Was she dreaming? Was this just a new, more terrifying nightmare? She dug her claws into the concrete path, but there was nothing to hold on to.

She bit, she scratched...

....she lashed at the thing that clung
to her leg.

But it didn't flinch. It heaved and pulled with overpowering strength, slowly dragging her back to the open catflap.

With a familiar click, the catflap door fell down. Over many years the edge of the flap had been worn to a fine, shiny finish — like a knife. As the lizard pulled, the edge of the flap dug into its hard, rubbery tongue.

On the other side of the catflap, the lizard howled with frustration and yanked hard, one last time.

Parsnip held her breath and waited for her awful end.

A second later, the sharp door sliced fully shut and the midnight air was filled with the lizard's pained cry.

The tongue's grip loosened. It peeled away from Parsnip's leg, then it shuddered and collapsed, lifeless in the dust. Parsnip could breathe again.

The Scaredy Cats stared at Kipling.
The hushed silence was broken by a
frightened mew behind them.

"I told you not to follow me!" Purdy
called angrily.

Fergal crept from his hiding place
into the secret circle. Purdy picked him
up by the scruff of his neck.

"This is no place for little kittens,"
Kipling said, fiercely. "The lizard could
be anywhere, waiting for tasty morsels
like you to walk past and flick-a-slick!"

"Ooooh!" cried Fergal. "I w-w-want
to go home!"

SCAREDY CATS

Shoo Rayner

❏ Frankatstein   1 84362 729 9   £3.99
❏ Foggy Moggy Inn   1 84362 730 2   £3.99
❏ Catula   1 84362 731 0   £3.99
❏ Catkin Farm   1 84362 732 9   £3.99
❏ Bluebeard's Cat   1 84362 733 7   £3.99
❏ The Killer Catflap   1 84362 744 2   £3.99
❏ Dr Catkyll and Mr Hyde   1 84362 745 0   £3.99
❏ Catnapped   1 84362 746 9   £3.99

Little HORRORS

❏ The Swamp Man   1 84121 646 1   £3.99
❏ The Pumpkin Man   1 84121 644 5   £3.99
❏ The Spider Man   1 84121 648 8   £3.99
❏ The Sand Man   1 84121 650 X   £3.99
❏ The Shadow Man   1 84362 021 X   £3.99
❏ The Bone Man   1 84362 010 3   £3.99
❏ The Snow Man   1 84362 009 X   £3.99
❏ The Bogey Man   1 84362 011 1   £3.99